RETURN OF THE
UNDERWEAR DRAGON

written by
SCOTT ROTHMAN

illustrations by
PETE OSWALD

RANDOM HOUSE STUDIO ▲ NEW YORK

Sir Cole needed an assistant knight.

So he wrote a letter to the kingdom:

Dear Kingdom,
I need an assistant knight. Applicants must be smart, hardworking, and eager to learn.
Please come to Camelot if you are interested. Ask for Sir Cole, because that's what they call me now.
—Sir Cole

The people of the kingdom read Sir Cole's letter and lined up outside Camelot. Apparently, lots of people want to be knights' assistants. . . .

Lady peasants with pheasants . . . giant monks with skunks . . .
jousting jugglers . . . scabbard smugglers . . .

beekeepers' sons . . . innkeepers' daughters . . .
makers of buns . . . twin candy hoarders . . .

As did a girl named Claire, who was preparing a kit for outwitting dragons in underwear.

Interviewing all of them was going to take Sir Cole forever.
So he went for a walk instead.

On his walk, Sir Cole kept seeing signs that reminded him of the Underwear Dragon.

And a thought suddenly hit Cole like a ton of medieval bricks.
The Underwear Dragon had entered the kingdom with his underwear
showing, then tried to destroy the kingdom, because . . .
he didn't know how to read!

So Sir Cole went
to find him.

Back in his cave, the Underwear Dragon was having a nightmare about Sir Cole.

But when he awoke and realized it was just a dream, the Underwear Dragon was super relieved but still worried.

He never wanted to see
Sir Cole again.

Unfortunately, Cole was knocking on his door.
"Hey, Underwear Dragon! It's Sir Cole! I know you destroyed the kingdom only because you couldn't read, so I'm here to teach you how!"

But the Underwear Dragon was too embarrassed to talk
to Sir Cole.
That's right. Underwear Dragons get embarrassed.

Underwear Dragons get embarrassed when they don't get gold stars . . .
can't do the monkey bars . . . trip on lutes . . .

accidentally toot . . . spill juice . . . grill Bruce . . . lose to Burt . . . stain their shirt . . .

meet someone new . . . step in poo . . . rip their shorts . . . are bad at sports . . .

crash down stairs . . . or lose their underwears.

The last thing the Underwear Dragon
wanted to do was admit he couldn't read.

So he pretended to be a duck.
"Sorry, the Underwear Dragon doesn't live here anymore. I'm just a giant duck, which you can tell is true because I speak fluent Duck. Quack quack! See? Go away now, please, Person I Don't Know!"

Sir Cole smiled. He had an idea.

"Well then, giant duck . . . maybe I can just teach YOU how to read, since the Underwear Dragon is definitely NOT here."

The Underwear Dragon had always wanted to learn to read,
and since he had such a great disguise, he said:

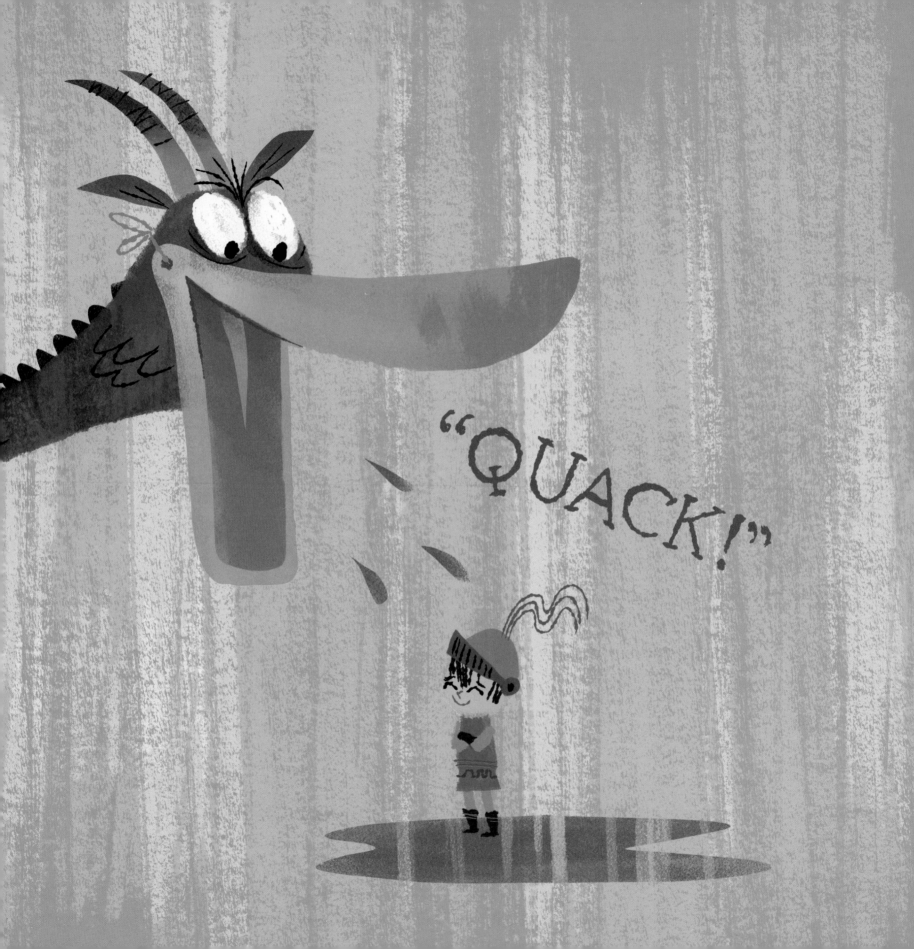

They started with the alphabet.

Then the sounds the letters made.

Next, some short words . . .

COOL

followed by longer ones.

Undrwhere

It was hard for both of them. Sir Cole wished he had an assistant to help.
Frustrated with himself, the Underwear Dragon took a deep breath . . .

. . . and torched the book they were using.

Then he went to destroy the kingdom again.

Cole was frustrated too. He wanted to give up.

But from out of nowhere, the girl named Claire
reached into the Outwit Dragon kit she had prepared . . .

. . . and pulled out a homemade fire extinguisher.
It gave Sir Cole an idea.

He found the Underwear Dragon just as he was about
to destroy the kingdom again . . .

. . . and gave him a new book he might like better.
The cool pictures greatly interested the Underwear Dragon,
and he calmed down.

So Sir Cole and the Underwear Dragon started over.

Whenever the Underwear Dragon got
frustrated and torched the book . . .

Claire just put the fire out.

The Underwear Dragon didn't give up this time. He kept trying . . . and trying . . .

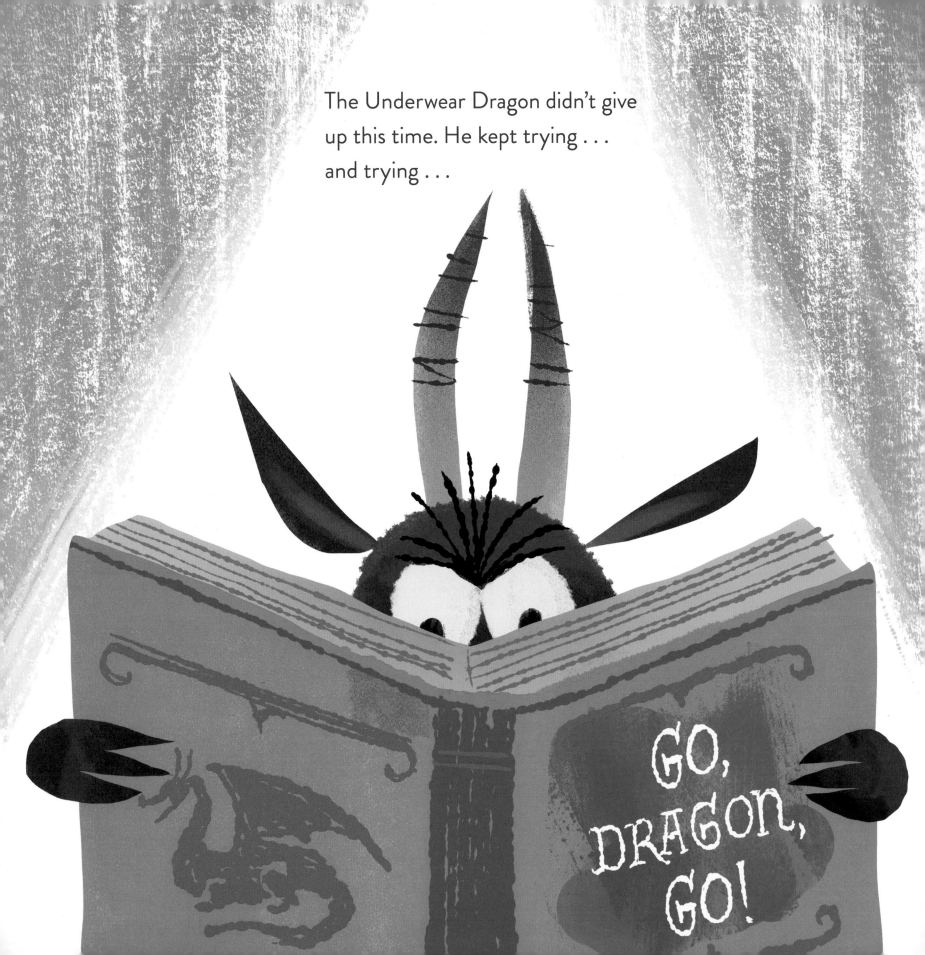

GO,
DRAGON,
GO!

until he learned how to read.

The Underwear Dragon felt fantastic, and Sir Cole gave him
a reward to show how proud he was of all his hard work.

Thanks to Sir Cole and Claire, the kingdom was saved and Claire was made his assistant knight.

The first thing Sir Cole asked Claire to do was write down everything that had happened to them so he could read the story every night . . . to every Knight of the Round Table.

To my parents, Nancy and Jeff
—S.R.

For Sam and Cuda
—P.O.

Text copyright © 2021 by Scott Rothman
Jacket art and interior illustrations copyright © 2021 by Pete Oswald

All rights reserved. Published in the United States by Random House Studio,
an imprint of Random House Children's Books, a division of Penguin Random House LLC, New York.

Random House Studio and the colophon are registered trademarks of Penguin Random House LLC.

Visit us on the Web! rhcbooks.com

Educators and librarians, for a variety of teaching tools, visit us at RHTeachersLibrarians.com

Library of Congress Cataloging-in-Publication Data
Names: Rothman, Scott, author. | Oswald, Pete, illustrator.
Title: Return of the Underwear Dragon / by Scott Rothman ; illustrated by Pete Oswald.
Description: First edition. | New York : Random House Studio, [2021] | Sequel to: Attack of the Underwear Dragon. | Audience: Ages 3–7. | Audience: Grades K–1. |
Summary: After realizing that the Underwear Dragon misbehaves only because he cannot read, Sir Cole and his would-be assistant, Claire, are determined to help the fearsome beast.
Identifiers: LCCN 2020052100 (print) | LCCN 2020052101 (ebook) | ISBN 978-0-593-11992-1 (hardcover) | ISBN 978-0-593-11993-8 (lib. bdg.) | ISBN 978-0-593-11994-5 (ebook)
Subjects: CYAC: Knights and knighthood—Fiction. | Literacy—Fiction. | Books and reading—Fiction. | Dragons—Fiction. | Apprentices—Fiction. | Humorous stories.
Classification: LCC PZ7.1.R762 Ret 2021 (print) | LCC PZ7.1.R762 (ebook) | DDC [E]—dc23

The text of this book is set in 18-point Brandon Grotesque Regular.
The illustrations were created using scanned gouache textures painted digitally in Photoshop.
Book design by Nicole de las Heras
MANUFACTURED IN CHINA
10 9 8 7 6 5 4 3 2 1
First Edition